Rosie Rudey

and the very Annoying Parent

in the same series

William Wobbly and the Very Bad Day
A story about when feelings become too big
Sarah Naish and Rosie Jefferies
Illustrated by Amy Farrell
ISBN 978 1 78592 151 3
eISBN 978 1 78450 411 3

Sophie Spikey Has a Very Big Problem
A story about refusing help and needing to be in control
Sarah Naish and Rosie Jefferies
Illustrated by Amy Farrell
ISBN 978 1 78592 141 4
eISBN 978 1 78450 415 1

Charley Chatty and the Wiggly Worry Worm
A story about insecurity and attention-seeking
Sarah Naish and Rosie Jefferies
Illustrated by Amy Farrell
ISBN 978 1 78592 149 0
eISBN 978 1 78450 410 6

Rosie Rudey
and the Very Annoying Parent

Sarah Naish and Rosie Jefferies

Illustrated by Amy Farrell

Jessica Kingsley Publishers
London and Philadelphia

First published in 2017
by Jessica Kingsley Publishers
73 Collier Street
London N1 9BE, UK
and
400 Market Street, Suite 400
Philadelphia, PA 19106, USA

www.jkp.com

Library of Congress Cataloging in Publication Data
A CIP catalog record for this book is available from the Library of Congress

British Library Cataloguing in Publication Data
A CIP catalogue record for this book is available from the British Library

ISBN 978 1 78592 150 6
eISBN 978 1 78450 412 0

Printed and bound in the UK

Meet Rosie Rudey and her family

Rosie Rudey lives with her mum, dad, brother William Wobbly, and sisters, Sophie Spikey and Charley Chatty. The children did not have an easy start in life and now live with their new mum and dad. All the stories are true stories. The children are real children who had difficult times, and were left feeling as if they could not trust grown-ups to sort anything out, or look after them properly. Sometimes the children were sad, sometimes very angry. Often they did things which upset other people but they did not understand why.

In this story, Rosie is feeling very annoyed by her parents! She is so annoyed that she has decided to run away. Rosie has a big thick shell around her to stop adults getting too close to her or helping her. What will she do now though? She has run away and can't ask anyone to help her out. Luckily, Rosie's new mum is good at finding the right words to help her find a way back home. Written by Rosie's mum, and Rosie (who is a grown-up now), this story will help everyone feel a bit better.

Rosie Rudey often had a grumpy, squished-up face.

She looked so fierce that other children (and even some grown-ups) were a bit scared of talking to her.

Rosie Rudey was pleased that other people crossed the street when they saw her coming. She thought, "Good, get out of my way!"

She didn't care that children quickly went to play somewhere else as she came near to them. She thought, "Keep away from me you stupid children!"

Rosie had been with her new mum and dad for quite a long time, but she still found them VERY annoying. They kept on telling her what to do...

"Rosie, put your coat on, it's cold outside."

"Rosie, bring your sandwich box to the kitchen, please."

"Rosie, stop being nasty to your brother."

VERY annoying indeed!

Rosie sometimes felt a bit like a tortoise. She made sure she had a big, fat, hard shell all around her, so no one could give her cuddles or make her feel sad anymore.

Her parents were VERY annoying because they didn't seem to take any notice of her grumpy, squished-up face, or her fat tortoise shell.

One day, Rosie had had enough of her annoying parents. She said to her mum, "That's it! I've had enough of you, always telling me what to do! I am running away!"

Mum looked out the window and said, "Oh dear, that's a bit sad. You must be feeling very cross to want to go when it's just about to rain."

"I don't CARE," said Rosie, in a very rude way.

Rosie stamped up the stairs. She stamped as hard as she could, so the stairs shook.

She went into her room and started pushing lots of things she needed into her bag. She packed her favourite teddy, some nice sparkly things for her hair, an apple and her pyjamas.

Mum came into Rosie's bedroom. She said, "I think you may need a warm jumper and a coat. It looks quite cold outside."

Rosie rudely snatched her bag off Mum and threw out the warm jumper.

"I don't care," she shouted. "I'm getting away from you."

Rosie stamped back down the stairs and marched out the front door, slamming it behind her.

She stomped along the pavement with a very grumpy face. She could feel her tortoise shell getting heavier and thicker.

After five minutes Rosie felt a bit tired, and a bit cold.

She wondered what her brother and sisters were having for tea.

She thought she might sneak back and have a look through the window.

When Rosie got back to the house, she tiptoed quietly up to the window and looked through.

She didn't see Mum using her 'slidey eyes' to notice Rosie by the window.

It looked to Rosie Rudey that EVERYONE was having a VERY NICE TIME WITHOUT HER! Rosie was very cross and made the most grumpy, squished-up face she had ever made.

"Right," she thought, "I am going to stay out all night, and make everyone cry and worry about me."

As it was a bit cold, Rosie thought she had best stay in the porch. No one would see her there. It was still cold in the porch though...and boring.

Rosie thought about the nice warm jumper her mum had tried to put in her bag. Her tortoise shell wasn't very warm, and it seemed to feel very heavy.

Suddenly, the door opened and stayed open a tiny bit. Rosie quickly folded her arms and made herself very small in the corner.

She made her fiercest face, tucking her head into her tortoise shell.

Rosie heard her mum talking to her dad.

She said, "I do hope Rosie will be able to come inside in the warm soon. It must be very difficult feeling so cross with your mum all the time. I will put her tea in the oven to keep warm."

Very slowly and carefully, Rosie peeped her head out of the tortoise shell.

She pushed the door open a bit further.

She could smell her favourite tea.

She could hear her brother and sisters playing.

No one seemed cross. It was all very strange.

Rosie tiptoed quietly into the hall and sneaked into the kitchen. Mum was in the kitchen.

She touched Rosie's shoulder and said, "Goodness me you feel a bit cold, let's make a nice hot drink for you."

The Rudey part of Rosie tried to push Mum's hand off, but luckily the Rosie part was in charge, so it stayed there. Nice and warm.

Mum sat with Rosie to eat her tea. Rosie thought her tortoise shell was very thin all of a sudden.

She didn't feel grumpy anymore, so very quickly Rosie looked at her mum and smiled.

Well, you never knew when the grumpy face was coming back, did you?

The End

A note for parents and carers, from the authors

This book was written to help you to help your child. All the children in the stories are based on real children and life events.

Rosie Rudey has many of the behavioural and emotional issues experienced by children who have suffered developmental trauma and therefore has attachment difficulties. You will see in this book that Rosie cannot trust adults, is angry with the world and is rejecting. You will notice how Rosie has a 'tortoise shell' to protect her from the needs and demands of others, and also works hard to prevent herself from attaching to her new parents, in the illustrations and story.

We provide training to parents, adopters and foster carers, who have said to us that they often feel out of their depth, and do not know what to say or do when faced with these issues. This story not only gives you valuable insight into *why* our children behave this way, but also enables you to read helpful words, through the therapeutic parent (Rosie's adoptive mum), to your own child.

This story not only names feelings for the child, but also gives parents and carers therapeutic parenting strategies within the story. The parent also names physical feelings. She tells Rosie she is cold as Rosie may be unaware of this. It features some techniques which you can try in your own family:

- **Giving space** – The parent waits patiently for the child to calm down and return to the family. She notices where the child is to keep her safe, but avoids confrontation as this would make Rosie feel ashamed and would escalate the situation.

- **Touch** – Many of our children function at a much younger emotional age, and never learned to control their emotions (self-regulate) as young babies. When our children are very upset, angry or spiralling out of control, simply placing a calm hand on their shoulder can help them to calm and to self-regulate. This kind of touch is not expected to be reciprocated. 'Mum' touches Rosie on her return, to connect and regulate.

- **Empathy and nurture** – Even when Rosie is very angry, the parent demonstrates empathy by offering a warm jumper and expressing concern about her daughter's well-being.

Sarah is a therapeutic parent of five adopted siblings, now all adults, former social worker and owner of an 'Outstanding' therapeutic fostering agency. Rosie is her daughter, and checked and amended Rosie's thoughts and expressed feelings to ensure they are as accurate a reflection as possible. Together, we now spend all our time training and helping parents, carers, social workers and other professionals to heal traumatised children.

Please use this story to make connections, explain behaviours, and build attachments between your child and yourself.

Therapeutic parenting makes everything possible.

Warmest regards,

Sarah Naish and Rosie Jefferies

If you liked Rosie Rudey, why not meet Callum Kindly, Charley Chatty, Katie Careful, Sophie Spikey and William Wobbly?

Callum Kindly and the Very Weird Child

A story about sharing your home with a new child

Rosie Rudey and the Enormous Chocolate Mountain

A story about hunger, overeating and using food for comfort

William Wobbly and the Very Bad Day

A story about when feelings become too big

Charley Chatty and the Disappearing Pennies

A story about lying and stealing

William Wobbly and the Mysterious Holey Jumper

A story about fear and coping

Katie Careful and the Very Sad Smile

A story about anxious and clingy behaviour

Charley Chatty and the Wiggly Worry Worm

A story about insecurity and attention-seeking

Sophie Spikey Has a Very Big Problem

A story about refusing help and needing to be in control